*Acting Edition*

# California

## by Trish Harnetiaux

ISBN 978-0-573-71175-6

www.concordtheatricals.com
www.concordtheatricals.co.uk

**FOR PRODUCTION INQUIRIES**

UNITED STATES AND CANADA
info@concordtheatricals.com
1-866-979-0447

UNITED KINGDOM AND EUROPE
licensing@concordtheatricals.co.uk
020-7054-7298

Each title is subject to availability from Concord Theatricals Corp.,
depending upon country of performance. Please be aware that
CALIFORNIA may not be licensed by Concord Theatricals Corp. in
your territory. Professional and amateur producers should contact the
nearest Concord Theatricals Corp. office or licensing partner to verify
availability.

This work is published by Samuel French, an imprint of Concord
Theatricals Corp.

No one shall make any changes in this title(s) for the purpose of production. No part of this book may be reproduced, stored in a retrieval system, scanned, uploaded, or transmitted in any form, by any means, now known or yet to be invented, including mechanical, electronic, digital, photocopying, recording, videotaping, or otherwise, without the prior written permission of the publisher. No one shall share this title(s), or any part of this title(s), through any social media or file hosting websites.

For all inquiries regarding motion picture, television, online/digital and other media rights, please contact Concord Theatricals Corp.

## MUSIC AND THIRD-PARTY MATERIALS USE NOTE

Licensees are solely responsible for obtaining formal written permission from copyright owners to use copyrighted music and/or other copyrighted third-party materials (e.g. artworks, logos) in the performance of this play and are strongly cautioned to do so. If no such permission is obtained by the licensee, then the licensee must use only original music and materials that the licensee owns and controls. Licensees are solely responsible and liable for clearances of all third-party copyrighted materials, including without limitation music, and shall indemnify the copyright owners of the play(s) and their licensing agent, Concord Theatricals Corp., against any costs, expenses, losses and liabilities arising from the use of such copyrighted third-party materials by licensees. For music, please contact the appropriate music licensing authority in your territory for the rights to any incidental music.

## IMPORTANT BILLING AND CREDIT REQUIREMENTS

If you have obtained performance rights to this title, please refer to your licensing agreement for important billing and credit requirements.

*CALIFORNIA* was first produced by Clubbed Thumb (Maria Striar, Artistic Director and Founder; Michael Bulger, Producing Director) at The Wild Project in New York City on May 20, 2022. The production was directed by Will Davis, with set design by dots, costume design by Mel Ng, lighting design by Oona Curley, and sound design by Leah Gelpe. The production stage manager was Diane Healy. The cast was as follows:

**MOM** . . . . . . . . . . . . . . . . . . . . . . . . . . . . . . . . . . . . . . . . . . . . . . . . . . . Annie Henk
**DAD** . . . . . . . . . . . . . . . . . . . . . . . . . . . . . . . . . . . . . . . . . . . . . . . . Pete Simpson
**ROB** . . . . . . . . . . . . . . . . . . . . . . . . . . . . . . . . . . . . . . . . . . . . . . . Jordan Bellows
**TUCKER** . . . . . . . . . . . . . . . . . . . . . . . . . . . . . . . . . . . . . . . . . . . . . Ethan Dubin
**LIZZIE** . . . . . . . . . . . . . . . . . . . . . . . . . . . . . . . . . . . . . . . . . . . Mallory Portnoy

# CHARACTERS

**MOM** – 40s or 50s or not

**DAD** – 40s or 50s or not

**ROB** – 16 or not

**TUCKER** – 14 or not

**LIZZIE** – 13 or not

# PARTS

## ONE
In the Driveway

## TWO
The Ridenhour Game

## THREE
*"Stranded and Alone"*

## FOUR
California

## FIVE
A Problem with Time and Space

# NOTE

The entire play happens in the car.
Basically.
You'll see.

# NOTE ON RADIO PLAY

A fully produced audio file of the radio play in Part Three is included with a license to produce *California*. This recording is optional.

# An Epilogue

**LIZZIE.**  Later,

and I mean years later,

even today, there's still a lot of uncertainty about exactly what went down.

For sure I had the most questions.

Maybe my brother Tucker?

It wasn't...Rob.

I don't blame my dad.

Though I'm pretty sure my mom does.

But since no one can find the tape,

which would have been proof,

it's impossible to know.

The one record is gone –

we'll have to recreate.

Door to door, from Spokane, Washington, to Huntington Beach, California, was over thirteen hundred miles. My dad was confident we could drive it in one shot. No stopping. It was important to leave early evening because it was summer, and the car had no air conditioning. Much cooler to drive in the dark. It would be roughly twenty hours straight, and a terrible idea.

We'd head west then turn south.

Eventually cross the Columbia River and continue through Eastern Oregon.

No one had told me about Eastern Oregon.

That it was not at all like Western Oregon.

It is flat, dry, strange.

I'm getting ahead of myself. We were near the Tri-Cities by the Hanford Nuclear Plant the first time death gets mentioned. No one tells you there will be a day when you realize you don't have much time left together...

Was this my day? Near Hanford, where once they accomplished the impossible?

It makes sense it was. But science *hadn't caught up yet.*

See, splitting the atom wasn't the miracle,

it was putting it back together.

Proving matter can exist in two places at once.

What if a story can split, just like the atom?

Does everyone live forever?

# ONE

## In the Driveway

\*\*

*(Distance driven: 0 miles.)*

*(Time spent in car: 4 minutes.)*

*(First landmark: Ritzville, Washington.)*

\*\*

*(The car is onstage, always.)*

**LIZZIE**. *(To audience.)* Still in the driveway.

*(Beat.)*

Sitting in the middle of the backseat is me.

Lizzie, thirteen. A terrible age that's frankly embarrassing to revisit.

She, I, hold a tape recorder.

> (**LIZZIE** *makes sure she is alone and hits play. It's a recording of her secretly singing something like the hit song from The Police, "Every Breath You Take." \* She likes it. She fast forwards a little and hits play to hear herself singing. She hits stop. Glances around, no sign of her brothers yet. She ejects the tape, flips it over, closes the cover and hits record.)*

---

\* A license to produce *California* does not include a performance license for "Every Breath You Take." The publisher and author suggest that the licensee contact ASCAP or BMI to ascertain the music publisher and contact such music publisher to license or acquire permission for performance of the song. If a license or permission is unattainable for "Every Breath You Take," the licensee may not use the song in *California*. For further information, please see the Music and Third-Party Materials Use Note on page iii.

*(She spends some time recording herself saying "I love you" a few different ways. She rewinds the tape and plays it back. Each time the recording says "I love you" she responds "I love you" back. This goes on until –)*

*(**TUCKER** gets in the car holding a book, the title visible,* The Oregon Trail. *A collage of brutally beaten and sliced body parts and wagon wheels on the cover. It's more violent than it should be. Or, actually, exactly as violent as it should be.)*

**TUCKER.** Tucker, fourteen-almost-fifteen, sits to her right.

Tucker knows better than to sit directly behind the driver.

Which will be his father.

*(**ROB** gets in the car, he wears eyeliner.)*

**ROB.** Rob, seventeen, sits to her left.

Many advantages come from sitting directly behind our father, the driver.

Most importantly: it's easier to avoid rearview mirror eye contact.

**LIZZIE.** Distance driven:

zero miles.

**TUCKER.** Time spent in car:

four minutes.

**ROB.** First landmark:

Ritzville, Washington.

61.7 miles away.

Don't let the name / fool you.

**LIZZIE.**  There is nothing remarkable about Ritzville.

Unless you count Spikes.

The home of remarkable Huckleberry / milkshakes.

**ROB & TUCKER.**  We never get to stop in Ritzville.

> *(A shift.)*
>
> *(They negotiate space, legs and arms finding their own places, definitely not wanting to touch one another even a tiny bit because of how gross that would be.)*
>
> *(For sure no one is, or has real plans to be, buckled up.)*

**ROB.**  I could give three fucks about California.

**LIZZIE.**  Grandpa and Grandma live there.

**ROB.**  No shit.

Who cares, Lizzie.

**LIZZIE.**  *They have cancer, Rob.*

/ Dad cares.

**TUCKER.**  *(Quieter.)* I'm sure Mom cares too.

**ROB.**  You have no idea what I'm talking about.

It's not *about* Grandma and Grandpa.

> *(Beat.)*

It's about having a voice

and it's about being heard.

Trust me. I'm *much older than you* / Lizzie.

**LIZZIE.**  You don't think I'd rather be going to the Poconos?

> *(**ROB** is fucking disgusted by her.)*

**ROB.** You have no idea *what* Poconos are –

**LIZZIE.** Ah, I do.

**ROB.** Or *where* Poconos are –

**TUCKER.** Sure she / does.

**LIZZIE.** New York *State.*

**ROB.** Tucker, run inside and grab Lizzie a trophy from my / trophy shelf.

**TUCKER.** You don't have a / trophy shelf.

> *(Each time **LIZZIE** says "Rob," **TUCKER** quietly echoes with a "Rob.")*

**LIZZIE.** Originally inhabited by the Iroquois, Rob.

Poconos have rolling hills and lakes and wildlife, Rob.

A long-ago destination for honeymooners, Rob.

Currently vacation home after vacation home, Rob.

Roadside ice cream, Rob.

> *(Beat.)*

Should I go / on, Rob?

**ROB.** Did you say something?

> *(**LIZZIE** looks out the back window... No parents yet.)*

> *(She lame-attempts to strap on her seatbelt, nope, won't buckle – whatever.)*

What are you looking for?

Why do you need so / much approval?

**LIZZIE.** Let's play The Ridenhour Game.

**TUCKER.** Not 'til Ritzville.

*(Holds up his book.)*

An entire family's about to be slaughtered.

**LIZZIE**. *Lucky family.*

> *(During the car trip, **TUCKER** will occasionally gasp at the horrors in his book. Mostly, he keeps his increasing uncomfortableness to himself because – even though he finds the adventurous-but-oft-doomed-family stories of early pioneers frightening – he feels exhilarated imagining he's in their place, fighting for self-survival and boldly disappearing into the unknown.)*

**ROB**. We only play to five.

**LIZZIE**. Six.

**ROB**. Five.

**LIZZIE**. Fine.

**TUCKER**. Double points for first name / last name.

**LIZZIE**. Yes.

**TUCKER**. Gene Ridenhour.

**ROB**. We know it's *Gene*, Tucker.

**LIZZIE**. Triple points if he mentions *college*.

**ROB**. When we hit five.

/ Game over.

**TUCKER**. Automatic win if he says *Gene Ridenhour* and *college* in the / same sentence.

**LIZZIE**. If I win,

If I win

If I win

If I win?

**LIZZIE.** I'm not sitting in the middle anymore.

**ROB.** Lame.

If I win,

neither of you

eat in the car.

**TUCKER.** Are you suggesting we starve?

**ROB.** *(Sniffs air.)* I'm suggesting it already smells like / Spam in here.

**TUCKER.** If I win...

**LIZZIE.** *(Concerned.)* Or...Doritos...

**TUCKER.** If I win Rob is silent through the entire state of Oregon.

**LIZZIE.** Good one.

Oregon's a pretty / BIG state.

**TUCKER.** Enormous.

**ROB.** *You two don't know about Oregon.*

**TUCKER.** Why do you think we don't know about geography? *We know the states*, Rob.

Stop insinuating that we have no, no knowledge of this very country in which we live.

**ROB.** Stop being / formal.

**TUCKER.** *It's* offensive.

*You're* offensive. / *Rob.*

**LIZZIE.** *Offensive.*

        (**ROB** *shrugs like it's his job. To the horror of* **ROB** *and* **TUCKER**, **LIZZIE** *opens a can of Coke.\**)

---

\* A license to produce *California* does not include a license to publicly display any branded logos or trademarked images. Licensees must acquire rights for any logos and/or images or create their own.

**TUCKER.** Woah, woah, woah –

    Easy on the liquids / *traveler.*

**ROB.** Are you trying to get us killed?

**LIZZIE.** What.

**TUCKER.** No *beverages* Lizzie.

**ROB.** Dad is NOT pulling over so you can / piss.

**TUCKER.** Use the facilities.

**LIZZIE.** I won't –

**ROB.** Ah, that's not how biology works.

**LIZZIE.** You got like a D in bee-ology Rob,

    forgive me if I don't look /

    to you for my bee-ology answers.

**TUCKER.** Lizzie, we haven't even left?

    We have a hundred thousand miles to traverse

    and you inexplicably have opened a *beverage* / while we are still *in the driveway.*

**LIZZIE.** Why are you saying "beverage" –

**ROB.** Your brother's right.

**TUCKER.** This is, is / mind blowing.

**LIZZIE.** Worry about yourselves.

**TUCKER.** There is *zero* chance we're stopping.

**ROB.** Zero chance.

**TUCKER.** Literally I just said that.

**ROB.** No stopping at all.

**TUCKER.** What reality are you in?

**LIZZIE.** *(To* **TUCKER.***)* Don't be such a nervous kid.

**ROB.** Reality's a construct.

*(Ugh, LIZZIE doesn't know where to set her Coke can now...)*

*(Eventually, gently, TUCKER can't help himself and helpfully takes it from her.)*

*(Hmm. He just holds it.)*

**LIZZIE.** Where are they?

**ROB.** What, scared?

**LIZZIE.** Why would I be scared?

**TUCKER.** Dad lost the map / or something.

**LIZZIE.** We don't need a map.

**ROB.** Our parents are Fossils.

**LIZZIE.** Washington.

Oregon.

*California.*

**TUCKER.** Have a little respect for Cartographers.

It's a special / skill?

**ROB.** Speaking of special.

Tucker, got some bad news for you, buddy.

**TUCKER.** *(Ignoring.)* Should we honk?

**ROB.** I was in Mom's room,

like in her closet looking through stuff,

and found all these old *newspaper clippings.*

*(Beat. Ugh, TUCKER bites –)*

**TUCKER.** So.

**ROB.** SO, they were like old. *Really old.*

So, I looked at them closer...and up near the top...was the *date.*

*The date of the clipping.*

**TUCKER**. Okay?

**ROB**. So – cheep, cheep, cheep – I do a little math and.

*(Beat. Ugh,* **TUCKER** *bites –)*

**TUCKER**. WHAT.

**LIZZIE**. You're pretty boring, Rob.

**ROB**. The date of the newspaper is exactly nine months before *your* birthday.

Your actual date of birth.

The day you came...out.
Of Mom.

**LIZZIE**.

And you know what? *Ewww – no one came out of Mom.*

**LIZZIE**. Or like, you're gross.

**TUCKER**. *No?*

**ROB**. The clippings were all about an explosion at an old aluminum plant in the valley.

Working with aluminum can be very, very dangerous, not everyone survives.

Especially when there's an explosion as big as this one.

**TUCKER**. Are you a metals expert / now?

**ROB**. There were fatalities.

One of the fatalities?

*(***LIZZIE*** gives tiny gasp.)*

A dude named TUCKER.

**TUCKER**. *What are you saying.*

*(***TUCKER*** starts to breathe hard.)*

**ROB.** I'm saying your REAL dad is most likely this dead aluminum plant worker named Tucker, dipshit. Not, say, our – *(His and* **LIZZIE***'s.)* dad. Like we all thought.

> *(Beat.)*

The name, *your name* – "Tucker" – was circled in creaky old red ink

and the paper was worn real thin. *Paper-thin.*

Probably from Mom's old tears or something.

> *(Beat.)*

Sorry you had to find out like this.

> **(TUCKER** *is breathing harder.)*

Pull it together, bro.

**TUCKER.** One day, Rob –

> **(LIZZIE** *hands* **TUCKER** *his inhaler from the seat pocket.)*

**ROB.** You sound like an asthma kid.

| **TUCKER.** | **LIZZIE.** |
|---|---|
| They're going to: Put. You. Away. | He IS an asthma kid. |

> **(TUCKER** *inhales deeply but turns so* **ROB** *can't watch.)*

**ROB.** Yikes.

I bet Dad doesn't even know.

> **(TUCKER** *concentrates his rage on Lizzie's Coke can.)*
>
> *(He opens the door and chucks it hard...)*

*(But it doesn't hit anything.)*

*(Only disappears.)*

*(Which is weird.)*

*(They all, privately, clock it.)*

*(Whatever.)*

*(**LIZZIE** leans forward and lays on the horn.)*

\*\*\*

*(A shift.)*

*(A later **TUCKER**, still holding the book.)*

**TUCKER**. As previously mentioned, I was *fourteen almost fifteen* and this trip was during – a *certain period* of schooling where they hit us *hard* with western expansion and life's terrible, irresponsibly documented inevitabilities *and* possibilities. I was there for it. I desperately wanted to freeze on a mountain pass. To watch my family starve to death. Unable to save them. Paralyzed by excitement and horror. I spent a fair amount of time privately selecting the best – and worst – ways to hypothetically self-perish.

*(Whispers.) Dysentery.*

*(Excited.)* I was concerned *and* relieved that eventually we all meet the same fate.

Comforted only by the understanding that, hell, I could change a fucking *wagon wheel* if I had to.

Lizzie and I have been comparing notes for decades. When I think about our drive to California, there's something about the actual Act of Driving that contributed to the split. Cutting through time and space. There's a world where none of this would have happened if we'd been on, say, a *Prairie Schooner*... but...then there wouldn't have been a radio. It was the radio, not the car, that was the catalyst.

None of us even liked our car...station wagon.

I'll tell you what we did like: our California grandparents, the ones we were going to see, had a vintage, ice blue Chevy van that everyone called The Blue Van Motel. *What??* Legendary. Sensational. Windowless.

It'll come up later...

    *(Beat.)*

Looking back, I will say this: *I'm the middle child.*

Even though I just talked a big game, like just now, a moment ago? The whole "everyone's dead, let's perish with honor" thing? I didn't *actually* want anything bad to happen.

    *(Indicates himself.)*

*Softie.* I'm a family guy. Everyone loves my wife – including me. I'd do anything for my kids.

I sit on numerous non-profit boards, change jobs every decade because I care about professional advancement and like my steak medium rare. I can ski well enough to actually go skiing, loved *Wicked* on Broadway and – hey – what are you doing in December, because Christmas is at *my* house.

I have a lot of heart.

Which is why it is so fucked up that I was the first to die.

# TWO

## The Ridenhour Game

\*\*

*(Distance driven: 160 miles.)*

*(Time spent in car: 2 hours 34 minutes.)*

*(Next landmark: Hanford Nuclear Power Plant, Washington State.)*

\*\*

**LIZZIE**. Distance driven: a hundred and sixty miles.

Time spent in car: two hours, thirty-four minutes.

Next landmark: Hanford Nuclear Power Plant, Washington State.

*(A shift.)*

*(**DAD** drives, reflecting on his entire life.)*

*(**MOM** sits shotgun engrossed in the huge map.)*

*(**KIDS** in the backseat, already super bored.)*

*(Oh god... **DAD** is sniffling.)*

*(**MOM** rubs his back and smiles in the mirror back at the kids.)*

**MOM**. Love you guys.

**ROB**. Dad, are you fucking crying?

**MOM**. Rob! /

Language.

**LIZZIE**. *stopitrob.*

**DAD**. *(Sniffles, wipes a tear.)* Just the damn ragweed, kiddo.

> *(No one believes him.)*

> *(**LIZZIE** leans up to **PARENTS**.)*

**LIZZIE**. Why do you let Rob talk / like that?

**DAD**. Like what, kitten?

**MOM**. *(Weirdly singing.)*
GOING-ON-A-ROAD-TRIP, A-ROAD-TRIP, A-ROAD-TRIP.

> *(Tries to get them to sing along.)*

GOING-ON-A-ROAD-TRIP, A-ROAD-TRIP –

**LIZZIE**. Mom, that's not like, *a song.*

> *(**MOM** already knew that.)*

**MOM**. It could be –

> *(**MOM** sees **TUCKER** tucked in his book, reading.)*

**DAD**. Your mom's a great singer.

**MOM**. Tucker, great skill. / Reading in the car.

**DAD**. *(Realization.)* My mom was a / terrible singer...

**MOM**. I get car sick.

> *(**TUCKER** shuts the book, suppressing the urge to panic.)*

**TUCKER**. Dad? Do we have a lot of meat in / the car?

> *(**DAD** has a fun idea.)*

**DAD**. Hey, let's all pretend we're / old friends!

**ROB**. "A lot of meat"?

**DAD**. We could just...laugh and laugh!

**LIZZIE**. "Old friends"?

**DAD**. Recall good times / from the past.

**LIZZIE**. You want to recall stuff?

**ROB**. Dad, do you have brain damage?

| **DAD**. | **TUCKER**. |
|---|---|
| Ha! | I think, as a family, we should ration / more. |

**MOM**. We have enough food, Tuck.

**TUCKER**. For emergency situations?

**MOM**. *(To **DAD**.)* It's okay to be a family. /

This *is* a *family* trip, honey.

**DAD**. Of course.

I was just... /

...thought...maybe fun...

**TUCKER**. Hello? Can anyone hear me? Meat update?

**ROB**. I'll give you a / meat update.

**MOM**. *(To **DAD**.)* Did you pack the meatloaf?

(**DAD** *winces.*)

| **LIZZIE**. | **DAD**. |
|---|---|
| Did you pack the ketchup? | Sure did. |

(**MOM** *doesn't believe him.*)

(*Flustered by his deceit,* **DAD** *accidently turns on the blinker.*)

(*This has happened before...the* **KIDS** *wait to see if he notices before –*)

**ROB, TUCKER & LIZZIE**.  Blinker.

> (**DAD** *turns off blinker.*)

> (*Beat.*)

**ROB**.  This seems fun, right Dad?

**LIZZIE**.  What's your idea of fun, Rob?

*Lighting things on FIRE?*

**DAD**.  (*Attempting cheer.*) It's fun / to pretend sometimes.

**ROB**.  Shut up, Lizzie.

/ That was an accident.

**MOM**.  (*To* **KIDS**.) That *was* an / accident.

**TUCKER**.  We can't say / "shut up."

**ROB**.  *It's over.*

**LIZZIE**.  Don't you mean "sealed."

**MOM**.  Almost!

/ Records seal the minute you turn eighteen.

**DAD**.  All I meant was pretending can be fun.

Takes your mind off things.

> (*Winks at* **TUCKER** *in the mirror.*)

Right, *Tuck*?

> (*OMG:* **TUCKER** *wants to die.*)

**TUCKER**.  Huh?

**DAD**.  I said, *it's fun to pretend sometimes* and that's *healthy.*

**ROB**.  *Pervert.*

> (*OMG:* **DAD** *is so embarrassing.*)

**TUCKER**.  Whatever, Dad.

*(Beat.)*

*(**ROB** stares at **TUCKER**. Then glances at **TUCKER**'s shoes.)*

*(Beat.)*

*(**ROB** won't stop staring at **TUCKER**. Then at his shoes.)*

**TUCKER**.  Stop staring at me.

**ROB**.  Just trying to figure you out, bro.

Just wanted to say, nice...Penny Loafers.

**TUCKER**.  *You wear eyeliner.*

> *(**TUCKER** looks out the window.)*

**LIZZIE**.  Cool pennies.

> *(**MOM** checks her watch.)*

**MOM**.  We're making great time.

I think we can do this in twenty / hours –

**DAD**.  Nineteen.

> *(**MOM** almost-laughs.)*

**MOM**.  If we never stop –

**DAD**.  Honestly?

**MOM**.  – that's not / realistic.

**DAD**.  Maybe even eighteen.

> *(**MOM** puts a soft hand on **DAD**.)*

**MOM**.  Remember...

> *(He does, but doesn't want to.)*

About expectations.

**DAD**. Mmm-hmm.

> *(If there's a window,* **TUCKER** *huffs on it, fogging it up.)*

> *(He writes their initials with a finger: T – L – R.)*

> *(If not, they find another way to keep score.)*

**LIZZIE**. Speaking of *meat* – Dad, after volleyball yesterday?

I was telling Jenny about your friend,

the one with the extreme taxidermy situation –

**DAD**. Gene.

Gene Ridenhour.

> *(Yes!* **LIZZIE** *quiet celebrates to self.)*

**LIZZIE**. Ridenhour, *right*.

> *(***TUCKER*** *puts two lines under the L.)*

**ROB**. But Dad –

**LIZZIE**. I mention because Jenny's against both *meat* and *fur*.

**ROB**. – who was the guy with the *chickens*?

**LIZZIE**. She was also disgusted Mr. Ridenhour's morbid collection featured / albino beavers.

**ROB**. That handed you a headless chicken that one time –

**DAD**. Ridenhour.

That was Ridenhour too.

That guy!

> *(***TUCKER*** *makes a face at* **ROB** *and puts only one line under the R.)*

**ROB**. Hey Dad, I'm happy to take over the driving later –

**LIZZIE & TUCKER.** Noooooo!

**ROB.** – if you get tired, or whatever.

**DAD.** Thanks, bud.

**ROB.** Thought I caught a yawn there.

**LIZZIE.** He didn't yawn.

> (**MOM** *gives* **ROB** *a wink in the rearview mirror.*)

**MOM.** You're a great driver, Rob.

/ Proud of you.

**TUCKER.** Dad didn't yawn.

Dad, did you yawn?

**DAD.** I think it was a smile?

> (**ROB** *smiles.*)

**ROB.** Know what?

I'm not annoyed we're on this trip.

It's good practice for the Cannonball Run.

> (**MOM***'s examining the map, looking for fun sites to point out.*)

**MOM.** What's that.

**ROB.** Just something we're doing.

**MOM.** We who?

**ROB.** Me and Kirk.

**MOM.** *(To* **ROB.***)* Kirk and I

**LIZZIE.** I hate / Kirk.

**TUCKER.** Kirk Burger's a dirtbag.

> (**TUCKER** *returns to his book.*)

**DAD.** Kirk Burger??

/ I went to law school with his dad.

**ROB.** Yeah.

**DAD.** Jared Burger... / unique fellow...

**ROB.** Anyway, it's a famous race thing.

**MOM.** *(Not a fan.)* Jared Burger was a hot shot.

**DAD.** Went into / personal injury...

**ROB.** Kirk told me about it. Dad, you'll like this – you drive from New York to L.A. in one shot.

Fast car, pack snacks, straight through.

> (**ROB** *fully expects his* **DAD** *to tell him how awesome that sounds...*)

**DAD.** Jared Burger, wow.

I have not thought of that guy in ages.

Kids, when I met your mother?

She was dating Jared Burger's younger brother, Derek Burger.

**MOM.** Derek Burger and I / went out twice.

**DAD.** Derek Burger was my roommate for a while. Real oddball. That whole family had real oddball energy.

They were all exceptionally INTO *Halloween*. Always dressing up and pulling pranks and eating candy. The Burger Brothers had big Halloween Energy... huh.

*(To* **MOM**.*)* Remember that?

**MOM.** I remember ditching Derek Burger to go on a drive with you.

> (**MOM** *and* **DAD** *laugh and laugh!*)

**DAD.** I used to say – hey, no one give that guy a gun!

*(MOM and DAD love the story of how Mom left Derek Burger to be with him for what turned out to be forever and how he'd tell everyone not to give Derek Burger a gun!)*

*(Beat.)*

*(LIZZIE turns to ROB.)*

**LIZZIE.** Your leg?

Is touching my leg.

**ROB.** It's not.

**LIZZIE.** *It is.*

And it's wet.

And sticky.

Before you drive from New York to L.A. with that loser Kirk Burger, can you wipe your leg off?

/ Mom, do you have a *Kleenex*?

**ROB.** *(Concerned.)* My leg is not wet Lizzie.

**LIZZIE.** I think it's really odd you *don't feel the moisture.*

*(TUCKER gasps at the book.)*

**ROB.** Just stop, Lizzie.

**LIZZIE.** If I hadn't been sitting next to you for the last few hours,

I'd be pretty sure that...*you'd just been swimming.*

It's like you crawled out of a lake.

*(Too loud.)* Mom??

**MOM.** Shh, I'm right / here –

**LIZZIE.** Do you have a *beach towel*?

*(MOM hands back some old car napkins.)*

(**ROB** *wipes his legs off with confused urgency.*)

**MOM**. Looks like we're about to go right by Hanford.

**LIZZIE**. Can we *speed* past Hanford?

**ROB**. Don't try to be / political, Lizzie.

**MOM**. It's a privilege Lizzie.

**LIZZIE**. I really don't crave radiation poisoning today.

**MOM**. Hanford did a lot of good.

**DAD**. Your mom's right.

**ROB**. Well, by "good" do you mean polluted the earth and killed a trillion people?

> (**TUCKER** *giggles at his book, pioneering's such a roller coaster!*)

**LIZZIE**. Pick a lane, Rob.

**MOM**. Kids –

**LIZZIE**. Mom, he's all over the place with his / belief systems.

**DAD**. Hey, Rob?

Do you like America?

And Freedom?

**ROB**. ...No.

> (**TUCKER** *abruptly shuts the book, whispering "brutal."*)

**LIZZIE**. *(To* **ROB**.*) Pathetic.*

*(To* **DAD**.*)* Dad, I like America *and* Freedom.

**DAD**. I know you do, kitten.

> *(Beat.)*

**LIZZIE**. So... I've decided not to answer to "kitten" anymore.

**DAD**.  Oh, alright... I can make...adjustment.

**MOM**.  Liz/zie.

**DAD**.  Lizzie.

(**MOM** *gives* **LIZZIE** *an understanding, proud smile.*)

(*They drive in silence for a while.*)

**TUCKER**.  Hey Dad, I wish we had one of those lawnmower car things –

**DAD**.  Tuck, I didn't know you liked to mow!

Ridenhour has one.

(**TUCKER** *puts a line under the T.*)

Maybe when we get back you can ride Gene's?

(**TUCKER** *adds another line.*)

I'm sure he'd teach you –

(**ROB** *fake coughs "bullshit" [like that part in* Top Gun *where Ice Man does it when Maverick's explaining how he was "inverted"], the "Gene" and the "Ridenhour" too far apart to count as double points.* **ROB-TUCKER** *stare off until –*)

(**LIZZIE** *points out the window.*)

**LIZZIE**.  Hanford sign.

**MOM**.  Plutonium has a place in our history.

**DAD**.  A real claim-to-fame.

**MOM**.  It's pretty cool *this* is where it happened,

considering how big the world is,

and here it was – mixed up in our own backyard.

**TUCKER.** Not sure they "mix it up" –

**MOM.** Sorry, Tuck – I mean this is where they synthesized Plutonium by taking Uranium-238, adding a neutron turning it into Uranium-239, then transforming it into Neptunium which, after some beta decay, becomes Plutonium...239. I mean, there's a lot more to it, but is that better?

**TUCKER.** *(Awe.)* That's *sick*, / Mom.

**ROB.** That's chemistry, right?

**DAD.** *(To* **MOM.***)* God, you're good at / science.

**LIZZIE.** Hey Mom – this could be a good job for you.

| **MOM.** | **DAD.** *(To self.)* |
|---|---|
| What / honey? | My mom was terrible at science... |

**ROB.** Excellent idea, Lizzie.

**LIZZIE.** Well, you're looking for a new job, right?

**MOM.** It's just a teachers' strike –

**LIZZIE.** How about Hanford Nuclear Power Plant Hostess –

**TUCKER.** Tour guide –

**LIZZIE.** Tour guide.

**ROB.** Escort?

**LIZZIE.** *Tour guide.* Hello, I'm Betty! / Welcome to Hanford.

**DAD.** Your mom has a degree in Psychology and a Minor in Spect... Spectros...copist...

**MOM.** Spectroscopy.

**DAD.** I can never / say that.

**MOM.** Nobody can. Just me.

**LIZZIE.** Hello, I'm Spectro-scop-op-olist Betty!

**ROB.** I bet you'd get a cool name tag too –

**LIZZIE**. Welcome to Hanford!

**ROB**. – like a diner waitress.

**MOM**. Nothing wrong with waitressing, Rob.

**LIZZIE**. A name tag would be great, but Mom – literally think how good you'd be at this. Imagine all these old, tarnished people in sweaters hobbling off tour busses and *you'd* be standing there. To greet them. You are very good at greeting. Completely put together, completely informed, and ready to like take them around and show them all the old, but still dangerous, probably leaking reactors.

> *(The three* **KIDS** *do a bad job at stifling their laughs.)*

**MOM**. Elizabeth.

**DAD**. Your mom can do anything.

**MOM**. Sweet to think of me, kids.

**DAD**. You should see her chop wood.

**MOM**. Let's not forget its monumental importance in our history

even if Hanford's a complicated place.

**TUCKER**. What's so / complicated.

**ROB**. Doesn't seem complicated.

**MOM**. Now, it's a problem to solve.

All that waste.

Storing it.

Disposing / of it.

**TUCKER**. Maybe Rob can help? He knows allll about storing waste.

*(To self.)* Good one, Tucker.

**DAD.**  Listen to your mother.

**MOM.**  Jobs are the core of / our economy.

**DAD.**  *(Self-muttering.)* I should have / listened to my mother...

| **LIZZIE.** | **TUCKER.** |
|---|---|
| Didn't everybody leave? | Isn't it slowly killing us? |

**MOM.**  It's a big part of the / community here.

**ROB.**  You love communities.

**DAD.**  Rob? Let's put it this way. We could – *Earth could* – be hit by an asteroid *at any moment.*

**ROB.**  Is this my fault?

**TUCKER.**  Not everything's / about you.

**DAD.**  Are you going to be mad at Space?

(**TUCKER** *returns to his book.*)

**LIZZIE.**  I don't think Rob's suggesting we get mad at space.

**ROB.**  Yeah, don't spin out, Dad.

**MOM.**  What are you suggesting, Rob?

**LIZZIE.**  It's all very...gross.

/ Gross to think about.

**ROB.**  What she said.

**LIZZIE.**  And, also? Gross in real life.

**ROB.**  *Thank* you, / sister.

**LIZZIE.**  It doesn't seem that arguing "job creation" is a good enough...nuclear forgiveness plan.

**ROB.**  See, this is what / I was saying.

**TUCKER.**  There is no such thing as a "nuclear forgiveness / plan."

**MOM**.  I appreciate I have children concerned about the environment.

**LIZZIE**.  Honestly, I'm only requesting we go a little faster.

/ In this part of our great country.

**DAD**.  …It's a bit of a speed trap around here –

**MOM**.  Ohh, I get it…

(*Rubs* **DAD**'*s neck.*)

Kids, your dad's having a *flashback*.

Remains haunted by that famous speeding ticket –

**DAD**.  I *was* thinking / about that –

**MOM**.  Who were you with?

**DAD**.  Gene Ridenhour. Back in college.

(*Boom!* **MOM** *slyly turns around and smiles at the* **KIDS**.)

(*Wow,* **MOM** *is way cooler than they thought.*)

(**TUCKER** *huffs on the window, adds an "M," and makes one big checkmark.*)

(**MOM** *holds up both hands putting her thumbs together and creating a "W." Winner.*)

It was so frustrating.

It was *Ridenhour* who liked to go fast.

But somehow, I was the one that ended up with the monster ticket.

(*This infuriates him.*)

*God Damnit.*

**LIZZIE**.  Back to Mom's future job opportunity –

*(Too far. **DAD** snaps.)*

**DAD.**  Instead of taking the piss out of your mother please *thank her* for the life she gave each of you.

Your grandmother lived in an orphanage, does that sound good?

Before that she lived in a car. Would you all like to live in a car?

*(**KIDS***: wait is this real? Yep.)*

*(**MOM** touches **DAD** in a soft, appreciative way the **KIDS** can't see.)*

...just...

*Just*...be better.

*(Beat.)*

*(<u>They really mean this:</u>)*

**LIZZIE.**  Thank you, Mom for the life you / gave me.

**ROB.**  You're the best / Mom.

**TUCKER.**  I appreciate you and also love you probably the / most Mom.

**ROB.**  Your generous smile makes me a / better person.

**LIZZIE.**  Every day, it's your love that holds our / family together.

**TUCKER.**  Your very presence calms my turbulent / heart.

**LIZZIE.**  If you somehow weren't my mom, I'd come / find you.

**TUCKER.**  You comfort me so I can live without / fear.

**ROB.**  I barely deserve you and all my friends think you're hot.

**MOM.**  *(To **DAD**.)* The cause of my misery, the source of my joy.

*(What did she say??)*

**LIZZIE.** Huh??

**MOM.** *Just talking to your dad.*

>    *(Beat.)*

**DAD.** Let's see what's on the radio.

>    *(**DAD** turns on the radio and shuffles through the AM stations as everyone settles in a bit more. He finds the perfect classical music and it fills the car.\*)*

>    *(The sun's been setting...the sky now a beautiful pink.)*

>    *(Apple trees now flank the road, branches almost extending over the car.)*

**MOM.** Apples!

**LIZZIE.** We could stop and pick some?

>    *(Everyone looks at **DAD**.)*

**DAD.** Well...

>    *(Everyone looks at **MOM**.)*

Gosh...

>    *(Everyone looks at **DAD**.)*

>    *(**DAD** panic glances at **MOM**.)*

>    *(**MOM** understands exactly what will happen, as if it's happened a million times before.)*

---

\* A license to produce *California* does not include a performance license for any third-party or copyrighted recordings. Licensees should create their own.

**MOM**.  What if we slow the car down, but never stop. Lizzie can sit on the windowsill. The boys will hold her legs...and she can reach up and pick the apples while we keep moving...but slower... then she'll hand them in through the window?

> (*Hmm...dangerous?*)

**DAD**.  And I keep driving, we keep going –

**MOM**.  Yes.

**ROB**.  You want us to dangle her / out the window?

**MOM**.  No one said / "dangle."

**DAD**.  This could work.

**LIZZIE**.  Rob's not touching / me.

**TUCKER**.  I can probably secure her.

**LIZZIE**.  Is it safe?

> (**DAD** *does like to live on the edge sometimes.*)

**DAD**.  Only one way to / find out.

**MOM**.  Let's make a "fun" memory!

> (**DAD** *hesitantly begins slowing as* **TUCKER** *rolls his window down.*)

> (**LIZZIE** *crawls over* **TUCKER**, *going headfirst out the window.*)

> (*She twists her body around [drawing on the one dance class she took] so she sits on the sill, holding the roof for balance.*)

> (*The apple branches pass by slow and beautiful.*)

> (*The wind on her face is heaven.*)

**LIZZIE.**  I'm alone...

I'm alone!

...This is all I've ever wanted...

*(A branch slaps **LIZZIE** on the head. It snaps loudly, but she's fine.)*

**MOM.**  All good up there?

**LIZZIE.**  *(For real!)* I've never felt more alive!

*(**LIZZIE** reaches, the timing right, and picks a perfect apple.)*

*(She tosses it in, hitting **ROB**.)*

**ROB.**  Ow, hey!

**LIZZIE.**  Oops! Sorry brother!

*(**LIZZIE** picks another perfect apple and hands it to **TUCKER** who gently hands it to **MOM**.)*

*(For a brief moment she considers her hand, it's taken her off guard, it looks like her mom's.)*

**DAD.**  Got one for your old man?

**LIZZIE.**  Coming up!

*(**LIZZIE**, back to never happier, picks an apple and hands it to **TUCKER** who hands it to **DAD**.)*

**DAD.**  *(Calling out to **LIZZIE**.)* Last one –

*(An extra-extra-large apple falls from a tree hitting the windshield, momentarily startling **DAD**, causing him to swerve the car. **LIZZIE** jerks hard but regains her balance.)*

TUCKER. *jesus christ.*

LIZZIE. I'm okay!

MOM. *(Come back in.)* Come on, Lizzie –

> *(She swipes one more before pulling herself back in the car, squishing* **TUCKER** *and settling back as* **ROB** *bites his apple.)*

> *(She lets him chew a sec before –)*

LIZZIE. What does a Nuclear Waste Apple taste like?

> *(***ROB*** *spits it out.)*

ROB. Mom!

TUCKER. Ha, Rob's gonna die.

MOM. We all die, Tuck.

/ Rob, you're fine.

LIZZIE. That was / awesome.

DAD. This apple is perfect.

> *(***DAD*** *bites into his apple.)*

LIZZIE. Can I do that again?

DAD. See?

> *(Chews...removes from his mouth.)*

/ Delicious.

ROB. Mom?

Aren't you going to eat yours?

MOM. I'm...

> *(Lying.)*

...allergic to apples.

You all know that.

I love peaches and pears!

If we pass a pear or peach orchard.

I'll eat one of those for sure.

      *(Weird, no one realized this... They drive on...)*

***

      *(A shift.)*

      *(The radio music distorts yet remains...as it should...that moment was decades ago...but also now.)*

**ROB**. If you're curious about that previous "Rob started a fire" business? Don't be. Yes, fine, sure, I take full responsibility, but my frontal cortex wasn't fully developed yet. This affects things like "the ability to plan" and "motivation" and "problem solving" – all important stuff.

So, actually, now that I'm saying this, I *don't* take full responsibility at all. It's science, it's in the books, get a library card if don't believe me. Read up. The fire was Kirk's idea anyway. The worse thing I did that year was quit my job at McDonald's to go tanning with the Altenruther twins.

There were a few years back then that I lost touch... that I'm not proud of... eventually I got everyone back. As my dad would say, even a blind hog finds an acorn once in a while. I *was* that blind hog but I found the acorn and went into finance – you should see my pool.

I was forty-five years old when my sister called late one night after our mom got sick to see if I remembered what exactly happened on the trip after Mom fell asleep (you'll see, she's about to). Lizzie wanted to know how I remembered it. And at first, I didn't. Hadn't really thought about it.

*(Beat.)*

Then as she was talking, I did.

Surprisingly clear...

*(...and unsettling.)*

Locking the doors.

Dogs barking.

The sharp shift to static.

The tape recorder.

The trailhead.

The rain and mud.

Tucker's shoe.

The footsteps...gaining...

See, in the car, during that time, I didn't understand my dad at all. Or what he was driving towards...

*(Tiny laugh.)*

I can still hear the tone of his voice when he said:

*Deal with it, Rob.*

*(Beat.)*

Please note, I never ate an apple again. Not the rest of my life. Not even in pie form.

To this day, I could tell you the story of what happened in Oregon. But I couldn't tell you for sure if we even made it to California.

**

*(A shift.)*

*(...Sixty miles later...)*

       *(**MOM** clutches the map.)*

**MOM**.  We're coming up on the river.

**DAD**.  Kids, the Umatilla / bridge.

**TUCKER**.  Where's the / state line?

       *(The **KIDS** adjust positioning, they know what this means.)*

**MOM**.  The state line's the very middle of the bridge.

       *(**MOM** stretches her left arm out in the center of the five of them, her hand in a fist.)*

       *(**EVERYONE** reaches to her fist, wrapping their hands around it.)*

**LIZZIE**.  Do we make a wish?

**MOM**.  We all / make a wish.

**LIZZIE**. *(Excited.)*        **DAD**.
All I want is to be /        Don't say it out loud!
(alone) –

**TUCKER**.  Here we go –

       *(They will hold this formation until they cross the border.)*

       *(This is normal and how they cross state lines in their family.)*

       *(No one ever thinks it's dumb or is too old or annoyed to enjoy it either.)*

       *(It's just something they all do. It's theirs.)*

**ROB**. *(To himself.)* My wish is so fucking good.

**DAD**.  Behold, Oregon!

## THREE

### *"Stranded and Alone"*

\*\*

*(Distance driven: 378 miles.)*

*(Time spent in car: 7 hours 43 minutes.)*

*(Next landmark: Crater Lake, Oregon.)*

\*\*

**LIZZIE.**  Distance driven: three hundred and seventy-eight miles.

Time spent in car: seven hours, forty-three minutes.

Next landmark – in a while – Crater Lake, Oregon.

> *(A shift.)*

> *(It's very dark by now.)*

> *(Classical music, both calm and tense, is still on the radio.)*

> *(On occasion, **DAD** hums along, trying terribly hard to appear present.)*

**TUCKER.**  What is Crater Lake.

**ROB.**  A lake. / In a crater.

**MOM.**  It'll be too dark to see.

**DAD.**  Fished it once with my dad… / stocked with kokanee.

**LIZZIE.**  Who even makes those decisions?

**MOM.**  Some say it's a sleeping volcano.

**TUCKER.**  "Some"…Cartographers?

**ROB**. Dude, we get it.

You / know the word Cartographers.

**DAD**. He wasn't great / at fishing…

**MOM**. It's the deepest lake in the U.S.

**LIZZIE**. But is it?

**DAD**. It's…just

*(Concerned.)* bottomless.

**LIZZIE**. I bet there's somewhere deeper. /

No one's discovered yet.

| **TUCKER**. | **ROB**. |
|---|---|
| Agree. | O-kay, Lizzie. |

      *(Beat.)*

**ROB**. Dad? Why is this crap still on the radio?

**TUCKER**. *you-suck-rob.*

      *(**TUCKER** flips on his flashlight and resumes reading.)*

**DAD**. This crap is soothing classical music, Rob.

**ROB**. No-thank-you, Father.

**MOM**. Don't call him Father.

**ROB**. What? Why?

**MOM**. He…prefers Dad.

**DAD**. I do. I called my dad, "Dad" – and you should call me "Dad."

**ROB**. Michael?

**DAD**. Or Michael, / Mike –

**LIZZIE**. Hey, Dad? Did your dad's dad call / his dad's dad "great-great-grand-dad"?

**MOM**.  Don't call him Michael.

**TUCKER**.  You missed a "great."

**DAD**.  Mom's right, just call me "Dad."

**MOM**.  Don't call me "Mom."

>      (**KIDS** *silent laugh.*)

>      (**DAD** *sighs. He would also probably close his eyes, but he's driving.*)

**DAD**.  Sorry.

**MOM**.  *I am not your mom.*

>      (**DAD** *absolutely knows she's not his mom. That she hates when he calls her "Mom" [even though "your mom" is fine] but now he can only sadly think of his mom. His knuckles tighten around the wheel.*)

**DAD**.  *(Whispering.)* ...I know.

**MOM**.  I only meant.

>      (*Beat.*)

  I'm exhausted.

**TUCKER**.  Being a mother seems exhausting.

**LIZZIE**.  Very tiring, agreed.

**ROB**.  Lizzie'll be asleep first.

**LIZZIE**.  I'm not / even tired.

**TUCKER**.  For sure.

**LIZZIE**.  *Mom.*

**MOM**.  Boys.

**ROB**.  Don't call us "boys."

**TUCKER**.  *(Quietly to* **ROB**.*)* Slay.

*(**DAD** starts channel surfing HARD on the radio.)*

*(...it's fuzzy,)*

*(then clear,)*

*( fuzzy then clear,)*

*( fuzzy – then CLEAR.)*

*(He lands on an old radio program mid-show –*)*

*(On radio, rain, a clap of thunder, more rain.)*

**DAD**.
Yessssss – we're in luck!

God, my parents loved *Stranded and Alone*.

*(**MOM** yawns.)*

**TUCKER**.
Like / conceptually?

**DAD**.
If I remember, a couple is in a car on a road trip.

**LIZZIE**. *(Gasps.)*
Kitten!

*(They listen.)*

*(**DAD**'s trying to remember more...)*

**WOMAN**.
Oh Randy, *this storm*.

**MAN**.
It's just nature, Janice.

Calm your nerves.

*Perfectly normal.*

**WOMAN**.
Why'd you take that shortcut?

It's so dark and stormy,

Do you even know where we are?

**MAN**.
I'm trying to get there faster, kitten.

**WOMAN**.
And now we're lost.

**MAN**.
You can't blame me –

---

* A fully produced audio file of the radio play is included with a license to produce *California*. This recording is optional.

(**DAD**'s *trying to remember more...*)

**DAD.** *(Remembers!)*
A murderer has escaped from a nearby asylum!

*(They listen.)*

**ROB.**
Dad, can we change –

**MOM.**
Rob – this stuff?

Stories and such?

Old sounds like these?

They're classics.

They're what make your dad happy.

*(They all listen.)*

*(**MOM** yawns again.)*

**WOMAN.**
Well, I do.

You're the one driving.

**MAN.**
You don't even *know* how to drive.

**WOMAN.**
Don't throw that in my face.

That's just like a man.

**MAN.**
I AM a man.

**WOMAN.**
I know darling, but I wish you had better instincts.

*(Clap of thunder.)*

**MAN.**
It's so dark, I hate it.

The trees are closing in –

**WOMAN.**
You're trying to scare me, Randy.

**MAN.**
It's...just...terribly hard to see.

**WOMAN.**
My nerves are already shot –

**MAN.**
I don't remember a forest on the map.

**WOMAN.**
Then why are there so many trees?

**MAN.**
Maybe we took a wrong turn...

**WOMAN.**
You don't know where we are?

**DAD.** *(Softly to her.)*
You can drift, we're good.

**MOM.**
You sure?

**DAD.** *(To **MOM**.)*
The kids are tired.

**ROB & TUCKER.**
No we're / not.

**LIZZIE.**
Nope.

*(Gratefully, **MOM** closes her eyes.)*

**DAD.** *(To radio.)*
They're going to run out of gas.

*(**MOM**'s breathing deepens almost immediately.)*

**TUCKER.**
Oh no.

*(**LIZZIE** gasps.)*

**DAD.**
Oh!

*(**DAD** rustles around, pulls out a box of graham crackers. He puts one in his mouth and awkwardly offers them back to the **KIDS**.)*

**MAN.**
I know where we're going.

And then we took the shortcut.

**WOMAN.**
Daddy always said there's no such thing as a shortcut.

**MAN.**
Well, Daddy's not here –

Look out!

*(A screech, sound of the car braking, swerving, trying not to hit something.)*

**WOMAN**
Oh my god,

What was that –

**MAN.**
I –

**WOMAN.**
What was that?

**MAN.**
Nothing, darling.

**WOMAN.**
Isn't that Institution around here?

*(Dramatic music.)*

We're so isolated.

**MAN.**
A road sign!

**DAD.**

Graham cracker?

(**ROB** *takes one absently as he listens.*)

(*The* **KIDS** *are into it now.*)

**LIZZIE.**

Mom's sleeping, should we turn it down?

**DAD.**

Your mom can sleep through anything.

(*They listen, intently.*)

**TUCKER.**

This isn't going to end well.

**LIZZIE.**

You would say that.

**ROB.**

You have no idea what humans are capable of.

**TUCKER.**

Fact: Everyone's capable / of Murder.

**DAD.**

Shhhhh.

---

(*The car slows down.*)

**MAN.**

Center Ridge Road.

**WOMAN.**

I think that Institution's on Center Ridge Road.

(*Clap of thunder.*)

**MAN.**

Damnit, it's getting harder to see by the second.

**WOMAN.**

Look! That sign! I knew The Institution was here... Just last week they locked up that awful old woman who killed all those children –

**MAN.**

She's locked up.

Besides, we're safe in the car.

(*Wonky car sounds...*)

Oh no...

**WOMAN.**

Randy, what?

(*The car putters to a stop.*)

**MAN.**

Well, I told you we should have stopped at the last gas station –

(*She gasps.*)

*(They listen.)*

**WOMAN**.
No!

**MAN**.
I'm afraid so.

**WOMAN**.
Oh Randy, what a place to run out of gas.

**LIZZIE**. *(Echoing.)*
*Oh Randy, what a place to run out of gas.*

*(Muffled sounds outside the car.)*

**MAN**.
Please be calm, Janice.

**ROB**. *(Echoing.)*
*Please be calm, Janice.*

**WOMAN**. *(Urgent whisper.)*
Turn off the headlights!

**MAN**.
What did you hear?

**WOMAN**.
Turn them off –

**MAN**.
What is it???

*(Beat.)*

*(All three **KIDS** are very into the story now, leaning forward, draped on the back of the front seat.)*

**WOMAN**.
Something...
I don't know.

**MAN**.
*Well stop.*
You're getting me all jittery.

*(**WOMAN** starts crying.)*
Stop trying to scare me... it's not fair...

**WOMAN**.
I keep hearing things.

**MAN**.
Rain. Animals. Nothing more –

(**TUCKER** *locks his door.*)

(**ROB** *locks his door.*)

(*A strange knocking in the car.*)

**TUCKER.**

Dad, speed up.

**DAD.**

Sure, bud.

(*A strange knocking in the car.*)

**ROB.**

What is that?

(*A strange knocking in the car.*)

**TUCKER.** (*Nervous.*)

What is it? It's not in the show –

(*The knocking starts again, louder. Then* **LIZZIE** *holds up* **ROB**'s *hand with a tight grip.*)

**LIZZIE.**

It's Rob's stupid hand.

**TUCKER.**

I hate you.

**ROB.**

Hate and love are the same emotion.

**WOMAN.**

Lock the doors!

**MAN.**

What did you see?

(*A sound.*)

**WOMAN.**

Lock them!

(*They both lock their doors.*)

You can't go out there, Randy.

**MAN.**

Okay, okay.

(*He doesn't believe this.*)

It'll be okay...

(*Muffled sounds.*)

**WOMAN.** (*Whispers.*)

Did you see that?

Someone's hiding in the woods.

**MAN.**

No one is hiding in the woods!

You're...you're mad, kitten.

(*She's a little loopy.*)

**WOMAN.**

I'm mad? You're the one driving us to that Institution all the way out here in the middle of nowhere...

You have a sickness, Randy...

**MAN.**

Oh sweetheart...maybe there's some happier music to play?

**DAD.**

Shhhhh –

*(They listen.)*

*(***MAN*** *looks for radio station, just like* ***DAD*** *did before... the same blips of stations...)*

**RADIO NEWS.**

– we're being told the Institution is in chaos... No electricity, a trail of dead in the halls and around the property. Authorities are having trouble with the search because of the rain and thunder and general terribleness of the storm. She was last seen fleeing towards Center Ridge Road and we regret to report a family was found slaughtered on the side of the road a mile from the Institution –

*(He turns the radio off. They listen to the rain beat down on the roof of the car.)*

**MAN.**

I can move fast, stick to the edge of the forest –

**WOMAN.**

No...no, Randy...

*(A barking.)*

*(Whispers.)* Randy – do you hear that?

**MAN.** *(Whispers.)*

What?

**WOMAN.**

Listen.

*(A dog barking.)*

Barking. It's barking. A dog?

**MAN.**

Janice –

(**ROB** *barks.*)

(**TUCKER** *barks.*)

(**LIZZIE** *barks.*)

(**DAD** *howls!*)

**WOMAN**.

Maybe there IS a house near!

(*A dog howling.*)

**MAN**.

I'll go.

I'll be as quiet as a mouse.

Quiet as a mouse...

**WOMAN**.

But that woman's out there.

(*Something slams against their car!*)

(**WOMAN** *screams!*)

That's her!

Do you see her –

Oh Randy!

(*They all jump!*)

**MAN**.

Oh darling, she has a –

(**ROB** *and* **TUCKER** *double check their door locks.*)

### (*THE STATION CUTS OUT AND GOES TO STATIC.*)

**DAD.** A cleaver! I swear she had a cleaver!

(*They listen.*)

*Shit.*

**ROB.** Whattttt / happened?

**DAD.** *Damn.*

**TUCKER.** Turn it back on!

**DAD.** (*Everything ends...*) We're out of range, bud.

**LIZZIE.** No!

**TUCKER.** Get it back –

**ROB.** Just find it –

**DAD.** It doesn't work like that –

**TUCKER.** Dad, get it back?

**ROB.** Massively disappointing. Father.

(**TUCKER** *frantically searches the backseat.*)

**DAD.** There's the beauty of AM radio at night.

The stations are unreliable.

Temporary...

(**DAD***'s shot back to thinking about their destination...*)

**TUCKER.** We need a better antenna.

*(Urgent.)* Maybe we can catch it –

(*He unrolls his window and holds out a different Coke can.*)

**DAD.** Not something to catch, Tuck.

(**ROB** *and* **LIZZIE** *search around,* **LIZZIE** *finds a metal hairbrush.*)

**LIZZIE.** This?

(**ROB** *grabs it, unrolls his window, and holds it out.*)

**DAD.** Guys, great effort –

I don't think –

**ROB.** Lizzie! Climb back out and hold the antenna –

**LIZZIE.** Okay –

(*She starts to climb back over* **TUCKER** *–)*

**DAD**.  Hey, *no, no, no.*

> (**LIZZIE** *stops.*)

Let me try one more thing –

> (*He channel surfs for a while without luck.*)

Sorry guys, it's gone.

> (*The* **BOYS** *roll up the windows.*)

> (**MOM** *murmurs though still fast asleep.*)

**TUCKER**.  How does it end?

**LIZZIE**.  Was it her?

Was it the / escaped murderer?

**DAD**.  I'm not sure –

**ROB**.  It had to be her –

**TUCKER**.  Dad, you can't, just, just suck us in to something like this and then...and then – *destroy us* by not letting us finish.

**DAD**.  Tuck, it's...the radio bud.

**LIZZIE**.  It's gone-gone?

**ROB**.  Pretty unfair.

**DAD**.  (*Sharp and mean.*) *Deal with it, Rob.*

> (*Silence.*)

> (*Regret.*)

> (*Silence.*)

Lizzie, did you bring the tape recorder?

**LIZZIE**.  Yes.

**DAD**.  All is not lost. When I –

*(The car lurches and flies suddenly, they've run over something.)*

*(**DAD** reflexively reaches an arm across sleeping **MOM** and for a swift and violent moment, he struggles for control, then regains it.)*

**LIZZIE**. *Oh my god.*

**DAD**. You guys / okay?

**ROB**. What did we hit –

**TUCKER**. Probably an / old man.

An old pioneer.

**DAD**. Sorry everyone.

*(He has no idea what they hit.)*

Probably a rabbit or a coyote.

Long dead. Saw it too late.

Everyone okay?

*(An unconvincing smattering of "yeah" "yes" "sure.")*

Your mom's a first-class sleeper.

A real champ.

**TUCKER**. Should we go back –

**ROB**. You heard the man. / *Roadkill.*

**DAD**. Tuck, it was partial.

Nothing we can do.

**TUCKER**. How can you be sure –

**DAD**. *(Hard pivot.)* So! When I was a kid, we'd make up stories –

(**KIDS** *groan.*)

**DAD**. We don't need the radio.

**ROB**. That show was actually good.

**DAD**. We have a tape recorder.

Our story will be better.

**TUCKER**. How?

**DAD**. We used to take these long trips with my folks in The Blue Van Motel –

*(They perk up at this mention.)*

– and we'd spin these wild stories.

Your grandfather had, *has*, an incredible deep voice.

We'd all play characters. Sound fun?

| **ROB.** | **TUCKER.** | **LIZZIE.** |
|---|---|---|
| If we do it can we get a dog? | Maybe. | What do we do? |

**DAD**. *We* finish the story.

**LIZZIE**. There's more of us. Five.

**ROB**. More like four –

**DAD**. So? We change it. It's ours now.

*(Gauging interest... they're listening.)*

Lizzie, is the tape at the very beginning?

**LIZZIE**. Hold please –

*(She rewinds the tape to the beginning.)*

Done!

**DAD**. Only ONE rule: you are no longer YOU.

**TUCKER**. Who are we?

**DAD**.  A version.

You're a version of you.

This takes full commitment.

No breaking.

**LIZZIE**.  What's breaking?

**DAD**.  Commit to anything that happens.

And to the version of you.

And to what happens to you.

That's the only way to get to the end.

**ROB**.  How do we know when it's over?

**DAD**.  We'll know.

> *(They nod, even though they don't understand.)*

Hit record, Lizzie.

> ***(She hits record.)***

> *(He puts on a stylized radio voice like the old radio program.)*

Good evening, and welcome to this evening's episode of *Stranded and Alone*.

**ROB**.  *(Earnestly.)* Sweet voice, Dad.

**DAD**.  If you're just tuning in,

we're afraid there's a bit of a situation...

...this one won't be a pleasant one folks...

It was a hot, dark summer night.

> *(They're into it.)*

> *(**MOM**'s deeply asleep, the map covers her like a blanket.)*

**DAD**.  A family of four –

**TUCKER**.  The mother had died.

> (**LIZZIE** *shoots him a look;* **DAD** *doesn't miss a beat.*)

**DAD**.  It was a hot, dark summer night.

A family of four, the mother having recently died,

had set out to make the long drive from Washington state to California –

**ROB**.  In The Blue Van Motel.

**DAD**.  It was a hot, dark summer night.

A family of four, the mother having recently died,

had set out to make the long drive from Washington state to California in The Blue Van Motel.

**TUCKER**.  In search of a new future.

**LIZZIE**.  It was raining.

**DAD**.  In search of a new future.

And it was raining.

> (**LIZZIE** *makes rain sounds to underscore.*)

The first hours of the trip had been perfectly normal.

Three teens, fighting in the backseat, munched on graham crackers,

unaware of the dimensional possibilities and about to confront their own mortality.

> (**TUCKER** *gives a quiet yet enthusiastic "Yes!"*)

Because shortly after the rain started,

somewhere in the desolate plains of Eastern Oregon,

something went terribly...horribly...wrong.

On a rural, desolate road, in the middle of nowhere –

The Blue Van Motel ran out of gas.

*Oh, dear.*

# FOUR

## California

**

*(Distance driven: ___ miles.)*

*(Time spent in car: ____ minutes.)*

*(Next landmark: _____.)*

*(Technically, physically, they are in the car still driving to California.)*

*(However, they are also in The Radio Show inside The Blue Van Motel, motionless and out of gas.)*

*(At first, any ambient sound effects [rain, thunder, lightning]* **come from the KIDS making the sounds...but soon sound effects become immersive, real. The audience enveloped in surround sound.***)*

*(All of Part Four is extremely heightened and deadly serious.)*

*(And yes, they are in character as a different version of themselves.)*

*(The tape recorder is ever-present.)*

**DAD.** Damnit, kids!

What a fine place to run out of gas.

**TUCKER.** We're going to miss her funeral.

**ROB.** Was the gas light broken?

**LIZZIE.** We know in our hearts, / she'd understand.

**DAD**.  No, no.

/ She'd never forgive us.

**ROB**.  I'd *hate* to miss her funeral.

She'd want / me there.

**TUCKER**.  She needs me there.

**LIZZIE**.  Are we still in Oregon?

**DAD**.  It *is* a big state.

**ROB**.  Hey –

> (*Shaking an invisible or visible compass.*)

– my compass isn't working.

Perhaps the weather?

> (**ROB** *does thunder.*)

**LIZZIE**.  If this is an electrical storm, which it is –

> (**TUCKER** *has a flashlight and does lightning.*
> *They take turns making "rain" sounds.*)

– then it must have thrown Earth's Magnetical Electrical Component *completely off course.*

**ROB**.  Which is exactly why my compass / wouldn't work.

**DAD**.  Excellent science, Lizzie.

**TUCKER**.  If only we were in a *Prairie Schooner*.

**DAD**.  Damnit to hell.

It's so dark now.

/ We should have driven during the day.

**TUCKER**.  One could say, *too* dark.

> (*Beat.*)

Perhaps there's an informative radio alert?

**DAD.** Great thought, son. I'll check. Meanwhile, Rob –

> *(**DAD** strips **MOM** of her map-blanket and hands it back to the **KIDS**.)*

> *(**DAD** **gently touches MOM, she turns slightly.**)*

– can you decipher this map?

**ROB.** For locational clues?

> *(**ROB** closely examines the large map with expertise.)*

**DAD.** Exactly, Rob.

**ROB.** I'll estimate the contour / intervals –

**LIZZIE.** Rob did get that A in / Map Class.

**ROB.** – and figure out the parallel latitudes.

**TUCKER.** Plus, Rob is a cartographer.

**DAD.** Estimate where *we* are and where the closest city *is*.

Then we can decide the best / route to take.

**ROB.** Sure, I'll just use radial-line plotting.

**LIZZIE.** It's most likely we'll need to take a trail up a steep mountain.

**TUCKER.** Dad, the radio? The update?

> *(**DAD** makes radio station changing sounds then finds the News Alert [he does this in a News Alert type voice].)*

**DAD.** – according to local authorities, the escapee, one Loretta McBeaver, has been missing for over three hours and considered terribly dangerous. Since breaking out of the institution she's left a trail of blood, death, and destruction. Every human being from The Dalles to Crater Lake should be on high alert. Lock the doors.

Close the shades. Do not leave your house. Do not travel. Keep off the roads... Stay safe out there, listeners.

(**DAD** *"turns radio off."*)

**TUCKER.** Ugh, *buffalo chips.*

**LIZZIE.** An unexpected dilemma for sure.

**ROB.** *(Consulting map.)* Family, we're definitely within the Danger Circumference.

I'd put us somewhere between Redmond and / Sisters.

**TUCKER.** High desert.

Lots of rocks.

**ROB.** Accordingly: we're about eight to twelve miles from the nearest village.

**DAD.** Great navigating, Rob.

> (**DAD** *tries to give* **ROB** *an encouraging smile,*
> *but* **ROB** *is busy navigating.*)

**LIZZIE.** There must be two / ways we can go.

**ROB.** It looks like there are two ways we can go.

**TUCKER.** Option one?

**ROB.** Option one: we take this road and walk twelve miles until we hit Redmond.

**LIZZIE.** Option two?

**ROB.** Option two: the high desert path towards Sisters.

As the crow flies –

**LIZZIE.** Is there a clear picture of the terrain?

**ROB.** Brother Tucker was correct: rocks, trees, mountains.

**DAD.** On foot, over the mountain IS fastest.

**LIZZIE.** And speed IS of the essence with this murderer on the loose.

**ROB.**  And a funeral to get to.

**TUCKER.**  Though with the rain, the trail could be / dangerous.

*(A shadow passes over.)*

**LIZZIE.**  Dad, kill the headlights.

Our young lives are at stake.

**ROB.**  As well as your old one!

**DAD.**  Point taken.

Alright –

(**DAD** *kills the headlights.*)

There, they're off.

*(It is much, much darker.)*

**ROB.**  I can't see.

**DAD.**  Because I killed / the headlights.

**TUCKER.**  I've lost all sight.

**DAD.**  Our eyes should adjust soon.

**LIZZIE.**  The path is our only, / only hope.

**TUCKER.**  Our brave sister is right.

We're sitting jackass / prey.

**DAD.**  There! See the trailhead between / those thick bushes.

**ROB.**  Game trail!

**DAD.**  We stay on the path, and we stick together.

**TUCKER.**  I'm worried about my choice of footwear –

**DAD.**  Tucker, please!

**ROB.**  Think of the greater good.

/ It's our only hope.

**TUCKER**. I'll quiet my discontent, brother.

**LIZZIE**. What a place to run out of gas.

**DAD**. We move as a unit. We move swiftly. We never take a cut-off.

I'll run vanguard. Lizzie behind me. Next, Tuck. Rob, bring up the rear.

*(They are ready, serious, excited.)*

**LIZZIE**. Cowabunga.

**TUCKER**. By the power of / Grayskull.

**ROB**. Remember the Alamo.

*(**Now, all sound elements become real. Ideally: the actors are mic'd, surround sound kicks in, the entire theatre is in the radio show.**)*

*(Car doors open, then shut.)*

*(Wind, rain, all sound elements are intensified.)*

*(They make their way to the trailhead.)*

*(Of course, in their physical reality, they remain in the car, driving.)*

**TUCKER**. *My shoe split –*

**DAD**. Clinch your toes / fierce, Tuck.

**LIZZIE**. The incline is steep

**ROB**. One foot in front of the other, Lizzie.

*(A branch snaps. A thud.)*

**TUCKER**. Lizzie! That branch hit me.

**LIZZIE**. Sorry!

**TUCKER.** I forgive you!

**DAD.** Keep your heads down –

**ROB.** Dad –

**DAD.** – *protect yourselves.*

> (*Climbing up the mountain, the trail narrows.*)

**ROB.** Dad –

**TUCKER.** ...My penny's gone! My toes punched / through my loafer –

**ROB.** Dad!

**LIZZIE.** It's getting so muddy –

**ROB.** Someone's behind me –

**DAD.** Just...a forest / creature –

**ROB.** Everyone, / *faster.*

**DAD.** Probably a rabbit, Rob!

**TUCKER.** It's getting slick –

**LIZZIE.** *Oh my god.* There's a drop off to one side.

**DAD.** Hug the mountainside, kids.

**TUCKER.** ...it's a full cliff...

**DAD.** We don't quit –

**TUCKER.** Dad... *Dad?*

**DAD.** *We just keep going.*

> (**DAD** *may whistle a few bars of "Bury Me Not on the Lone Prairie," underscores until he speaks again.*)

**ROB.** Family, we *got this* –

**TUCKER.** Oh, hair in the butter!

*(Confusing sounds.)*

Oh no –

*(**TUCKER** slips from the trail and falls off the cliff.)*

Daaaaaaadd/dddddddddd –

**ROB**. He's / falling –

**LIZZIE**. Tucker?!

*(**TUCKER**'s screams fade as he falls hundreds of feet to the scree below.)*

*(A broken thud. More rain.)*

*(**TUCKER** remains motionless in the backseat.)*

**DAD**. Tuck?

Tucker!

*(So very scared.)*

Keep going / other kids.

**LIZZIE**. We have to / help him –

**ROB**. N*o time*, Lizzie.

**DAD**. For the good of the many –

/ For the good of the many –

**ROB**. It's gaining... it's no rabbit... it's her, she's coming in hot!

*(Their footsteps pick up, they are moving quicker.)*

**DAD**. There's a glow of light over the next ridge!

**LIZZIE**. Where –

**DAD**. It must be / the village.

**ROB.** Sisters!

**LIZZIE.** *Civilization.*

**ROB.** Faster, Lizzie –

**DAD.** Stay the course –

**LIZZIE.** Stick together –

**ROB.** We can make it –

> *(They continue climbing and reach a fork in the path.)*

**DAD.** A fork... the path splits...

Both narrow... let's try the left...

oh wait... *what...*

oh no

wait

*damnit*

oh no

wait... what

wait – oh no!!

Ahhhhhhhh.

> *(A large tree falls, crushing* **DAD**.*)*

> *(***DAD*** remains motionless while driving.)*

**LIZZIE.** Dad?

Dad?

Dad?

Dad?

Dad?

*(**DAD** is silent because he is dead.)*

**ROB**. *(Urgent whisper.)* Right, Lizzie, go right! / Lizzie –

**LIZZIE**. But Rob?

**ROB**. *GO.*

**LIZZIE**. Okay –

Dad –

Tucker –

**ROB**. I see the light too –

*(**ROB** is lying, he doesn't see the light.)*

*(Behind him, the footsteps are gaining.)*

**LIZZIE**. You do?

**ROB**. Just ahead!

Keep going!

*(The footsteps are closer.)*

*(**LIZZIE** looks back –)*

**LIZZIE**. Is she behind you?

**ROB**. Don't look back, go –

*(**ROB**'s grabbed from behind. Muffled screams, struggle, confusion… nothing.)*

*(Only **LIZZIE** now. Running.)*

*(Everyone else motionless.)*

**LIZZIE**. Rob?

Rob?

Rob?

Rob?

**LIZZIE**.  Rob?

Rob?

Rob?

Rob?

>   (**LIZZIE** *running and running and running.*)
>
>   (*Branches break.*)
>
>   (*Rain slamming down from above.*)
>
>   (*Flashes of lightning [A stranger's face in a flash, then gone].*)
>
>   (***A shift... Her voice has a slight echo... she's in a new place...***)

Hello?

Anyone?

Can you hear me?

Dad?

Tuck?

*You guys this isn't funny.*

**MOM?**

HELLO???????????????????

I see it –

**Just a bit further –**

*Come on, Lizzie.*

>   (*A distant/distorted sob is heard, it's* **TUCKER**.)

*Come on, Lizzie.*

*(Another distant/distorted sob is heard, poor* **ROB.***)*

**Come on, Lizzie.**

*(Still another distant/distorted sob is heard.)*

*(It's* **DAD***... He's trying to be so quiet [but is so unsuccessful].)*

*(***LIZZIE** *fights to control her breathing.)*

*(Finally, she hits stop on the tape recorder.)*

*(***We snap back to before. No rain. No running.***)*

*(***Headlights pop on. Radio pops on. The car is in motion.***)*

*(***DAD** *and* **ROB** *and* **TUCKER** *shake quietly with their sobs.)*

*(***LIZZIE** *fights to control her hard breathing...)*

*(***MOM***'s arms stretch wide... she yawns awake with a satisfied, post-nap smile.)*

*(Unaware of the state of the others, she peers through the windshield and smiles.)*

**MOM**.  *(Not quite awake.)* Kids, look!

*(Looking ahead.)*

The state line.

## FIVE

## A Problem with Time and Space

*(A glitch. A shift.)*

*(There is a tremendous visual adjustment.)*

*(Physically, all of them are in the car, in the positions they were at the top of Part Four.)*

*(But everyone except* **MOM** *is now in flat, monochromatic yellow light.)*

*(***MOM*** puts on lipstick in the rearview mirror. The bus is almost here, she wants to look her best.)*

*(***MOM*** is much older now [hell, it's decades later!] and super cheerful.)*

*(She looks around.)*

*(She pins a name tag to the top right of her shirt, it says BETTY.)*

*(Oh, great. Everyone's here.)*

**MOM.** Hello, everyone!

*(From this moment on, two scenarios happen at once – proving there is no stronger bond than familial entanglement.)*

*(One:* **MOM** *gives the audience a tour of the Hanford Nuclear Plant.)*

*(Two:* **DAD**, **ROB**, **TUCKER** *and* **LIZZIE** *repeat [though it's the first time too] their version of the radio show with the precise choreography of Part Four.)*

*(Though we see their lips moving, we can't hear them... how could we?)*

*(We're in the other dimension.)*

***(Dimensional intersections (bolded) should link up [action moved accordingly].)***

*(\*Confession: The timing will be tricky between* **MOM***'s dialogue and the reenactment. Do the best you can, there's an extra verse of the song to use if necessary.)*

*(***MOM*** sure asks a lot of questions but never waits for any answers.)*

On behalf of The United States Department of Energy, the good ole DOE, welcome to the Hanford Nuclear Plant. These days, she likes to be called – the Hanford Site.

I'm Betty, but you can call me Betty.

> *(Beat.)*

My daughter told me that would get a laugh.

Hope the bus ride wasn't too long.

Look around. This place changed the world. How often can you say that? You're encouraged to reflect on the crucial work the DOE accomplished as one would reflect on, say, childhood. Not everything will make sense. If you're confused, call your brothers.

Remember when we all did things like drive to California? We have Hanford to thank. →

**DAD**.
> Damnit, kids!
>
> What a fine place to run out of gas.

There's no shame in having complex feelings full of contradiction! It's inescapable, so whether you're here because your parents made you come or here to celebrate or condemn the ethical choices made by the scientific community, remember there's not many of us who understand what we're even *doing*. Ever.

Many of the original Hanford employees didn't even know what they were working on! They just... kept going. It's so important to remember what you're smelling isn't a rotting mishandled hydrogen sulfur compound – it's Love. Family. Forgiveness.

**TUCKER**.

We're going to miss her funeral.

**ROB**.

Was the gas light broken?

**LIZZIE**.

We know in our hearts, / she'd understand.

**DAD**.

No, no.

/ She'd never forgive us.

**ROB**.

I'd *hate* to miss her funeral.

She'd want / me there.

**TUCKER**.

She needs me there.

**LIZZIE**.

Are we still in Oregon?

**DAD**.

It *is* a big state.

**ROB**.

Hey –

> *(Shaking an invisible or visible compass.)*

– my compass isn't working.

Perhaps the weather?

> (**ROB** *does thunder.*)

**LIZZIE**.

If this is an electrical storm, which it is –

> (**TUCKER** *has a flashlight and does lightning. They take turns making "rain" sounds.)*

I'm sure lots of you brought snacks. *Nourishment.* Eat Up and Clean Up – your mess. Please don't touch anything since this is already the most toxic place in America.

– then it must have thrown Earth's Magnetical Electrical Component *completely off course.*

**ROB**.
Which is exactly why my compass / wouldn't work.

**DAD**.
Excellent science, Lizzie.

**TUCKER**.
If only we were in a *Prairie Schooner.*

**DAD**.
Damnit to hell. It's so dark now. / We should have driven during the day.

**TUCKER**.
One could say, *too* dark.

Perhaps there's an informative radio alert?

**DAD**.
Great thought, son. I'll check. Meanwhile, Rob –

> *(***DAD*** strips* ***MOM*** *of her map-blanket and hands it back to the* ***KIDS****.)*

*(***MOM*** *turns slightly with the touch.)*

← *(***DAD*** *gently touches* ***MOM****, she turns slightly.)*

*(***MOM*** *smiles at a very personal memory.)*

– can you decipher this map?

**ROB**.
For locational clues?

> *(***ROB*** *closely examines the large map with expertise.)*

Guess how many reactors there are – yep, nine. Who knows how many buildings there are? 554 buildings. *Great job.* With so many buildings, you're probably

**DAD**.
Exactly, Rob.

thinking how easily people got lost, but it's true what they say – sometimes a perspective shift is all it takes. One of the major things Hanford has taught us is that nothing ever goes away. Plus, there's usually someone near to help! Think of the workforce it took to keep this place chugging. The key to creating any strong workforce or economy or family is... anyone? Yes! It's fear.

I know, easy for me to say. I can sleep through anything, but I always know where my family is.

Some quick housekeeping – in the unlikely event of an emergency, find the nearest windowless room, close your eyes, and *hold* one another. Whisper secrets, embrace confessionalism,

**ROB**.
  I'll estimate the contour / intervals –

**LIZZIE**.
  Rob did get that A in / Map Class.

**ROB**.
  – and figure out the parallel latitudes.

**TUCKER**.
  Plus, Rob is a cartographer.

**DAD**.
  Estimate where *we* are and where the closest city *is*.

  Then we can decide the best / route to take.

**ROB**.
  Sure, I'll just use radial-line plotting.

**LIZZIE**.
  It's most likely we'll need to take a trail up a steep mountain.

**TUCKER**.
  Dad, the radio? The update?

  (**DAD** *makes radio station changing sounds then finds the News Alert [he does this in a News Alert type voice].*)

**DAD**.
  – according to local authorities, the escapee, one Loretta McBeaver, has been missing for over three hours and considered terribly dangerous. Since breaking out of the institution she's left a trail of blood, death, and destruction.

understand *who* you're dying with. Ask yourself, what's a life?

Fact: the plutonium made at the Hanford Nuclear Plant in Eastern Washington was used in creating the second nuclear bomb dropped on Japan in Nagasaki. Do you think the second bomb was necessary?

You think everything is only and always happening to you? That you kids are the first of your kind? Pioneers? That your dad's need to hurtle towards his past in order to be in the present is easy? Being drawn *while* repulsed by the growing stench of what he'll face in Huntington Beach? He knows what he's in for when we finally pull into his parents' driveway. Don't we all?

Every human being from The Dalles to Crater Lake should be on high alert. Lock the doors. Close the shades. Do not leave your house. Do not travel. Keep off the roads... Stay safe out there, listeners.

*(***DAD*** "turns radio off.")*

**TUCKER**.
Ugh, *buffalo chips*.

**LIZZIE**.
An unexpected dilemma for sure.

**ROB**. *(Consulting map.)*
Family, we're definitely within the Danger Circumference.

I'd put us somewhere between Redmond and / Sisters.

**TUCKER**.
High desert.

Lots of rocks.

**ROB**.
Accordingly: we're about eight to twelve miles from the nearest village.

**DAD**.
Great navigating, Rob.

*(They share a smile.)*

**LIZZIE**.
There must be two / ways we can go.

**ROB**.
It looks like there are two ways we can go.

**TUCKER**.
Option one?

This is why it's important to take an extra moment... it's okay to get lost staring at the desert. It's okay to be still and count succulents or gaze at palm trees. That's exactly how the Hanford scientists would unwind back when this was a working power plant. They'd lose themselves, mesmerized by mirages floating on top of sand and dirt, lost in quiet thought and in no way thinking of all our future health issues.

Which is exactly why we sat so long in the driveway when we pulled up to your grandparents' house. He wasn't trying to make you crazy. Sitting in a driveway is sometimes necessary. It was about protection – his, yours, mine – the minute a car door opens everything's real. Right?

**(MOM** *glances up.)*

**ROB**.

Option one: we take this road and walk twelve miles until we hit Redmond.

**LIZZIE**.

Option two?

**ROB**.

Option two: the high desert path towards Sisters.

As the crow flies –

**LIZZIE**.

Is there a clear picture of the terrain?

**ROB**.

Brother Tucker was correct: rocks, trees, mountains.

**DAD**.

On foot, over the mountain IS fastest.

**LIZZIE**.

And speed IS of the essence with this murderer on the loose.

**ROB**.

And a funeral to get to.

**TUCKER**.

Though with the rain, the trail could be / dangerous.

← *(A shadow passes over.)*

**LIZZIE**.

Dad, kill the headlights.

Our young lives are at stake.

**ROB**.

As well as your old one!

Did you know a desert is just another kind of driveway? This is one of the reasons I became a Hanford Tour Guide. So I could let you know there's nothing wrong with spending hours in the car staring out the window. That you can be alone – together. I'm not an expert, but I do know that uncertainty's part of the job.

And now I'd love to share with you an old trail song from the west. We love our ballads, as I'm sure you do.

*(She now has a ukulele or some small instrument and starts strumming.)*

This one's called "Bury Me Not on the Lone Prairie."

*(MOM smiles and strums.)*

**DAD**.

Point taken.

Alright –

*(**DAD** kills the headlights.)*

There, they're off.

*(It is much, much darker.)*

**ROB**.

I can't see.

**DAD**.

Because I killed / the headlights.

**TUCKER**.

I've lost all sight.

**DAD**.

Our eyes should adjust soon.

**LIZZIE**.

The path is our only, / only hope.

**TUCKER**.

Our brave sister is right.

We're sitting jackass / prey.

**DAD**.

There! See the trailhead between / those thick bushes.

**ROB**.

Game trail!

**DAD**.

We stay on the path, and we stick together.

**TUCKER**.

I'm worried about my choice of footwear –

**DAD**.

Tucker, please!

*(Singing.)*

OH, BURY ME NOT ON THE
    LONE PRAIRIE
THESE WORDS CAME LOW
    AND MOURNFULLY
FROM THE PALLID LIPS OF A
    YOUTH WHO LAY
ON THE BLOODY GROUND
    AT THE CLOSE OF DAY


(**MOM** *keeps
strumming.*)


This one's for all you peanut
butter lovers... Liquid waste
isn't as scary as it sounds –
actually it looks and feels
like *peanut butter.*

**ROB.**

Think of the greater good.

/ It's our only hope.

**TUCKER.**

I'll quiet my discontent, brother.

**LIZZIE.**

What a place to run out of gas.

**DAD.**

We move as a unit. We move
swiftly. We never take a cut-off.

I'll run vanguard. Lizzie behind
me. Next, Tuck. Rob, bring up
the rear.

*(They are ready, serious,
excited.)*

**LIZZIE.**

Cowabunga.

**TUCKER.**

By the power of / Grayskull.

**ROB.**

Remember the Alamo.

**TUCKER.**

*My shoe split –*

**DAD.**

Clinch your toes / fierce, Tuck.

**LIZZIE.**

The incline is steep.

**ROB.**

One foot in front of the other,
Lizzie.

*(A branch snaps. A thud.)*

**TUCKER.**

Lizzie! That branch hit me.

*(Singing.)*
OH, BURY ME NOT AND HIS
    VOICE FAILED THERE
BUT WE TOOK NO HEED TO
    HIS DYING PRAYER
IN A NARROW GRAVE JUST
    SIX BY THREE
WE BURIED HIM THERE ON
    THE LONE PRAIRIE

*(**MOM** keeps
strumming.)*

**LIZZIE**.
    Sorry!

**TUCKER**.
    I forgive you!

**DAD**.
    Keep your heads down –

**ROB**.
    Dad –

**DAD**.
    *– protect yourselves.*
        *(Climbing up the mountain,
        the trail narrows.)*

**ROB**.
    Dad –

**TUCKER**.
    ...My penny's gone! My toes
    punched / through my loafer –

**ROB**.
    Dad!

**LIZZIE**.
    It's getting so muddy –

**ROB**.
    Someone's behind me –

**DAD**.
    Just...a forest / creature –

**ROB**.
    Everyone, / *faster.*

**DAD**.
    Probably a rabbit, Rob!

**TUCKER**.
    It's getting slick –

*(Extra verse if necessary, singing.)*

(OH, BURY ME NOT ON THE LONE PRAIRIE
WHERE THE COYOTES HOWL AND THE WIND BLOWS FREE
WHERE THERE'S NOT A SOUL THAT WILL CARE FOR ME
OH, BURY ME NOT ON THE LONE PRAIRIE)

*(**MOM** keeps strumming.)*

*(**MOM** singles someone out.)*

**MOM.**

You remind me of my son.

**TUCKER.**

This is the part when Tucker dies.

*(He joins **MOM** in the new light.)*

Mom...what's happening?

**LIZZIE.**

*Oh my god.* There's a drop off to one side.

**DAD.**

Hug the mountainside, kids.

**TUCKER.**

...it's a full cliff...

**DAD.**

We don't quit –

**TUCKER.**

Dad... *Dad?*

**DAD.**

*We just keep going.*

*(**DAD** whistles a few more bars of "Bury Me Not on the Lone Prairie"...)*

**ROB.**

Family, we *got this* –

**TUCKER.**

Oh, hair in the butter!

*(Confusing sounds.)*

Oh no –

← *(**TUCKER** slips from the trail and falls off the cliff.)*

Daaaaaaadd/ddddddddddd –

**ROB.**

He's / falling –

**LIZZIE.**

Tucker?!

*(**TUCKER**'s screams fade as he falls hundreds of feet to the scree below.)*

*(A broken thud. More rain.)*

**MOM.**

I found your penny!

*(She sets her uke down – but the song continues – as she hands him the penny.)*

**TUCKER.**

I'm fourteen traveling to California… I am scared of the future –

**MOM.**

Thinking the worst is ahead dismisses the fact that the worst has already happened. *Focus on what's beautiful.*

**TUCKER.**

I'm twenty-six, my daughter's born… We have no idea what we're doing… My wife has saved my life… We are in Spokane, Livingston, Great Falls. Then down to Portland, Bend, Salem. Spokane, Seattle. There are now five of us!

**MOM.**

There's always been five of you, like there's always five of us.

**DAD.**

Tuck?

Tucker!

*(So very scared.)*

Keep going / other kids.

**LIZZIE.**

We have to / help him –

**ROB.**

No *time*, Lizzie.

**DAD.**

For the good of the many –

/ For the good of the many –

**ROB.**

It's gaining… it's no rabbit… it's her, she's coming in hot!

**DAD.**

There's a glow of light over the next ridge!

**LIZZIE.**

Where –

**DAD.**

It must be / the village.

**ROB.**

Sisters!

**LIZZIE.**

*Civilization.*

**ROB.**

Faster, Lizzie –

**DAD.**

Stay the course –

**LIZZIE.**

Stick together –

**ROB**.

  We can make it –

    *(They continue climbing and reach a fork in the path.)*

**DAD**.

  A fork... the path splits...

  Both narrow... let's try the left...

  oh wait... *what*...

  oh no

  wait

  *damnit*

  oh no

  wait... what

  wait – **oh no!!**

  Ahhhhhhhh.

*(MOM singles someone out.)*

**MOM**.

  Hey – my husband had that sweater!  ←  *(A large tree falls, crushing* **DAD**.*)*

    *(***DAD*** *remains motionless while driving.)*

*(***TUCKER*** *finds comfort in this.)*

**DAD**.

  This is the part when Dad dies.

*(He joins* **MOM** *and* **TUCKER** *in the new light.)*

**LIZZIE**.

  Dad?

  Dad?

  Dad?

  Dad?

  Dad?

  Dad?

**MOM**. *(Lovingly.)*

  Perfect timing.

    *(***DAD*** *is silent because he is dead.)*

*(Ah, he understands everything.)*

**DAD.**

Have you always known?

*(It's been a long time since* **TUCKER***'s seen his* **DAD***.)*

**TUCKER.**

...Hey, Dad.

**DAD.**

Hey, Tuck!

I was driving the family to California...

not realizing *I was always in California*!

**MOM.**

Someone's paying attention ☺

**DAD.**

It's 1963. I'm fifteen, dreaming of heading north. Washington state. My desire to go *north* as a teenager intersects with my desire to go *south* as an adult – meeting in the middle, in Oregon. Incredibly, journeys seemingly in competition with each other, only occurring because of each other.

**ROB.** *(Urgent whisper.)*

Right, Lizzie, go right! / Lizzie –

**LIZZIE.**

But Rob?

**ROB.**

*GO.*

**LIZZIE.**

Okay –

Dad –

Tucker –

**ROB.**

I see the light too –

*(***ROB*** is lying, he doesn't see the light. Footsteps gaining.)*

**LIZZIE.**

You do?

**ROB.**

Just ahead!

Keep going!

*(The footsteps are closer.)*

*(***LIZZIE*** looks back –)*

**LIZZIE.**

Is she behind you?

(**MOM** *singles someone out.*)

**MOM.**

And you, little man, remind me of my other son!

←

**ROB.**

This is the part when Rob dies.

(**ROB** *joins* **MOM** *and* **TUCKER** *and* **DAD** *in the new light.*)

(**DAD** *laughs with understanding.*)

**DAD.**

Why do we think there's such a thing as a straight line?

**MOM.** *(To* **ROB.***)*

Hi, honey.

**ROB.**

Mom? I'm seventeen and fifty-three...

**ROB.**

Don't look back, go –

(**ROB**'s *grabbed from behind. Muffled screams, struggle, confusion... nothing. Only* **LIZZIE** *now. Running. Everyone else motionless.*)

**LIZZIE.**

Rob?

Rob?

Rob?

Rob?

Rob?

Rob?

Rob?

Rob?

(**LIZZIE** *running and running and running.*)

(*Branches break.*)

(*Rain slamming down from above.*)

(*Flashes of lightning.*)

(*A stranger's face in a flash, then gone.*)

(*A shift... Her voice has a slight echo... she's in a new place...*)

Hello?

Anyone?

Can you hear me?

Dad?

**TUCKER.**

I'm an old man...

**DAD.**

Look at you, Tuck.

**MOM.**

**I can see it!**          →

**ROB.**

Dad, I eat graham
crackers all the time.

**DAD.**

Aren't they / great?

**TUCKER.**

Where's Lizzie?

**ROB.**

I love to listen to AM
radio.

**MOM.**

She's almost here –

**Just a bit further,**     →
**Lizzie!**

**ROB.**

Especially after...
my father died...

**DAD.**

I'm right here, bud.

**MOM.**

**Come on, Lizzie!**       →

**ROB.** *(To everyone.)*

I miss you.

**TUCKER.** *(To everyone.)*

I miss you.

---

Tuck?

*You guys this isn't funny.*

MOM?

HELLO????????????????????

*(We hear* **LIZZIE.***)*

I see it –

*(We hear* **LIZZIE.***)*

Just a bit further –

*Come on, Lizzie.*

*Come on, Lizzie.*

*(We hear* **LIZZIE.***)*

*Come on, Lizzie.*

MOM.
Everyone, stop feeling so alone! 28 million baby salmon are born each year right here in this stretch of the Columbia River! It's okay, we're all here.

(**LIZZIE** *hits stop on the tape recorder.*)

(*A shift.*)

(*The radio pops back on with the same classical music as long before.*)

(*We are back in the car in the moment we left at the end of Part Four...though something has shifted... no one is crying or upset... there's a new sense of understanding and realization...and wonder.*)

(**MOM** *moments from waking up.*)

LIZZIE.  (*Quietly.*) I love you.

(**TUCKER** *puts a hand on* **LIZZIE**.)

TUCKER.  We're okay.

LIZZIE.  I love you.

ROB.  (*To* **LIZZIE**.) We're all here.

(**DAD** *is feeling all his feelings at once.*)

(*He is also feeling thirsty.*)

(*He understands what he needs to do.*)

**DAD.** Who's thirsty?

> *([Normally against policy]* **DAD** *gives everyone a Coke.)*

> *(Wow, the* **KIDS** *can't quite believe they get Cokes.)*

**TUCKER.** Really?

> *(Everyone opens their Cokes.)*

> *(***MOM** *stretches her arms and yawns awake.)*

> *(***MOM** *peers through the windshield and smiles.)*

**MOM.** Kids, look –

The state line.

> *(As the California state line draws close, a different sort of unity transforms them.)*

> *(***MOM** *stretches her left arm out in the center of the five of them, her hand in a fist. Everyone reaches to her fist, wrapping their hands around it. They will hold this until they cross the border. This is normal, how they cross state lines in their family.)*

> *(No one ever thinks it's dumb or is too old or annoyed to enjoy it either. It's just something they all do. It's theirs. And that's cool.)*

> *(There's the feeling that, even if this is it, even if this is the end, it's okay. They'll find each other again.)*

> *(Each of them understanding this wish will be very different from their last wish.)*

**LIZZIE.** *California.*

> *(As they cross the California state line they are engulfed in a white light.)*
>
> *(And disappear.)*
>
> *(This has been a plutonium comedy.)*
>
> *(Thank you for coming.)*

## The End